DIVING OFF THE EDGE

BY JAKE MADDOX

illustrated by Sean Tiffany

text by Bob Temple

STONE ARCH BOOKS

Impact Books are published by Stone Arch Books
151 Good Counsel Drive, P.O. Box 669
Mankato, Minnesota 56002
www.stonearchbooks.com

Library of Congress Cataloging-in-Publication Data
Maddox, Jake.
    Diving off the Edge / by Jake Maddox; illustrated by Sean Tiffany.
    p. cm. — (Impact Books. A Jake Maddox Sports Story)
    ISBN 978-1-4342-1205-4 (library binding)
    ISBN 978-1-4342-1398-3 (pbk.)
    [1. Swimming—Fiction. 2. Best friends—Fiction. 3. Friendship—
Fiction.] I. Tiffany, Sean, ill. II. Title.
PZ7.M25643Di 2009
[Fic]—dc22   2008031954

Summary:
Riley and Blake have been best friends forever, even though Blake is a
daredevil and teases Riley. That all ends when Blake finds a new group
of friends. Riley joins the swim team and soon finds he doesn't need
Blake's friendship to get by. But when Blake tries a crazy stunt at the
lake one day, can Riley put the past aside and save his former friend?

Creative Director: Heather Kindseth
Graphic Designer: Carla Zetina-Yglesias

1 2 3 4 5 6 14 13 12 11 10 09

TABLE OF CONTENTS

CHAPTER 1

Riley peered out over the edge of the cliff. Far down below, he saw his friends splashing around in the water.

"Come on, Riley!" one of them yelled. "Jump already! Everybody else did!"

Riley knew his friend was right. One by one, all of his friends had leapt off the cliff that hung over the bay in Lake Owens. One by one, they had splashed happily into the water below.

Riley was the only one of them who had not done the big jump before. Now, he was the only one still standing on the cliff.

Riley inched his toes forward and peered down toward the water. *It's so far down there,* he thought. *What if I hit a rock under the water or something?*

He tried to calm down, but he could not get his brain to stop worrying.

"Do you need me to come up there and hold your hand?" yelled Riley's friend Blake. Riley could hear all the other guys laughing.

For years, Riley had watched people jump off the cliff into the lake. It was something people did every summer once they were teenagers. Riley had never done it, but it seemed like everyone he knew had.

Blake had started jumping the year before. This year, he'd convinced Riley to try.

Riley had never seen anyone get hurt, but he had heard the stories. There was one kid in the 1980s who dove head-first, hit a rock underwater, and was paralyzed. There was another kid who didn't jump far enough to land in the deep water. He broke three bones.

When he was a little kid, Riley never thought he'd be afraid to make the leap. Everyone's parents said to stay away from the cliff at Lake Owens. But that never stopped anyone. Every year, people headed out to the lake, ready to take their chances jumping off the dangerous cliff.

His friends had started planning their jumps as soon as the weather warmed up.

That's when Riley started to get nervous. When the plans finally had been made the week before, Riley was scared.

Riley hadn't said anything, though. He didn't want his friends to think he was a chicken.

When Riley and his friends reached the cliff, Blake was the first one to jump. Riley wasn't surprised. Blake always had more courage than everyone else.

That wasn't always a good thing. For as long as Riley had known Blake, Blake had always been the kind of guy who got in trouble by trying things he shouldn't have. Sometimes it just seemed as if he liked acting tough or cool. Riley was much more cautious, but he and Blake were still best friends.

Down below the cliff, Riley saw Blake get out of the water. He started to climb up to the cliff again. Riley was sure Blake was planning to push him off.

Riley sighed. He didn't want to jump. He just wanted to get down into the water. He loved swimming. Being in the water was one of Riley's favorite things.

Blake was getting closer. Riley inched to the edge of the cliff. Slowly, he closed his eyes and bent his knees. Then he jumped off the side of the cliff.

CHAPTER 2

Riley felt the air rush up around him. He heard his friends' excited yells from the lake below.

Down, down he fell. The fall seemed to last forever. He kept his eyes squeezed shut. But as he felt the water getting closer, he opened his eyes. Just as he did, he felt the pain. It was sharp, like a knife, but it covered his entire back. Riley heard the horrible *smack!*

If he hadn't immediately sunk into the water, Riley would have thought that he had landed on solid ground. The pain across his back felt like a thousand sharp little pins.

Riley popped back above the water and gasped for air. He let out a horrible groan. All of his friends swam over, laughing hysterically.

"That was awesome!" one of them said. "I've never seen someone land flat on his back in the lake before!"

"I've never heard a noise that loud!" another one said. "It was like a gunshot!"

The pain from hitting the water started to go away. Riley tried to smile along with his friends. Mostly, he was just really glad it was over.

Riley had finally jumped off the cliff. Now his friends would stop making fun of him, and he could just have fun swimming in the lake.

Riley and his friends spent the rest of the day clowning around in the water. Blake jumped off the cliff a few more times, but nobody asked why Riley didn't want to jump again. It was a perfect spring day.

* * *

The next morning, Riley headed to school. His gym class was the first class of the day. It was his least favorite class.

Riley didn't think he was any good at sports. He hated basketball and football. He hated baseball and soccer. And as much as Riley loved to be in the water, he hated swimming at school.

That day was the second day of the swimming unit in gym class. Riley was not looking forward to it.

Riley and Blake were in the same gym class. It was the only class they had together. They met at Blake's locker before class and walked to the pool together.

"I really hate gym class," Riley complained to Blake. "We don't ever get to play any games in the pool or try diving or anything. We always have to learn all these stupid strokes and practice them, over and over. It's like Mr. Casey doesn't want us to have any fun, ever."

Mr. Casey was the gym teacher. He was also the swim team's coach. Riley figured that was why the teacher always made them practice the boring stuff.

Blake shook his head. "We should just skip first period," he said. "It's so boring. We can just hang out until second period starts."

Riley rolled his eyes. "Swimming is boring, but I'd rather be bored swimming than be bored in detention after school," he said.

"Whatever, chicken," Blake said. He smiled and added, "I guess you're right."

I can't imagine how much trouble that kid would get in if it weren't for me, Riley thought, shaking his head.

CHAPTER 3

OFF TO THE RACES

In the pool locker room, Riley and Blake changed into their swimsuits. Then they walked through the showers to the pool. When class started, Mr. Casey gathered everyone at the deep end of the pool.

"Today we're going to do something a little different," Mr. Casey said. "First, you're all going to learn how to jump off the starting blocks. Then we're going to have some races."

Most of the class groaned at Mr. Casey's announcement. But Riley smiled. For some reason, he actually felt excited. He was glad to be doing something other than practicing swimming strokes.

Blake looked at him and rolled his eyes. "Oh, great," Blake said. "We should have skipped class after all."

"Hey, at least we get to do something different today," Riley said, shrugging.

Mr. Casey taught them some different ways to jump off the starting blocks. Each student took a turn going off the blocks.

"Don't go too deep into the water," Mr. Casey said. "Stay close to the top of the water's surface. Then you'll lose less energy before your first stroke, and you'll be able to go faster."

"What strokes do we have to use for the race?" a kid asked.

"Our races today will be freestyle," Mr. Casey replied.

Blake blurted out, "Great! That means we get to do whatever we want!"

"Actually, no," Mr. Casey said. "Freestyle means you will be swimming the front crawl. That's the most basic stroke in swimming. We went over it last week, remember?"

A few of the other kids laughed. Blake shrugged. "Yeah, I guess," he said.

"How long are the races?" another kid asked.

"The pool is 25 yards long. The shortest race will be 50 yards, from one end of the pool to the other and back," Mr. Casey said.

"Got it," the kid said.

"Those short races are called sprints," Mr. Casey said. "Some races during our swim meets are as long as 400 yards. That's a total of sixteen times across the pool!"

"Sign me up for the sprints," Riley said. "I want to go fast."

"Everyone will get a chance to try a short race and a long race today," Mr. Casey said. "I'll tell you more about the long race in a while. First, let's work on turns."

Mr. Casey taught the class how to do a kick turn at the far end of the pool. A kick turn allowed the swimmers to spin underwater and kick off the end of the pool. Then they could change directions without stopping.

To his surprise, Riley really liked the kick turns. When he was swimming for fun, he loved doing tricks under water. The kick turns reminded him of that feeling.

After a while, Mr. Casey blew his whistle. "All right," he said. "I need six swimmers for the first sprint race."

Riley and five other swimmers raised their hands. "Get on your blocks," Mr. Casey told them.

When the swimmers were ready, Mr. Casey yelled, "Three, two, one. Go!"

Riley was the first one off the blocks. He swam as hard as he could. He quickly reached the end of the pool and turned around using a kick turn.

Then he started to feel tired. His legs felt heavy, and it was hard to move his arms.

Finally, he finished the race.

Gasping for breath, Riley looked up. He was in fifth place. He slapped the water in disgust.

CHAPTER 4

DISTANCE SWIMMER?

As Riley climbed out of the pool, Mr. Casey walked up. "Don't worry, Riley," Mr. Casey said, smiling. "Something tells me you'd be better as a distance swimmer."

"What do you mean?" Riley asked.

Mr. Casey replied, "I think you could be a good long-distance swimmer. You'd just need to learn to pace yourself."

"Oh," Riley said. "Well, I'll see what happens in the long race, I guess."

Riley watched as Blake raced in the 50-yard race. Blake won first place.

Riley sighed. Blake was really courageous. He always believed he could do whatever he wanted. Sometimes that got him in trouble. But other times, it helped him win.

I wish I was more like that, Riley thought.

Finally, it was Riley's chance to try a distance race. "Let's get started," Mr. Casey said. "We'll begin with the same group who started the short race. Each race will be 200 yards. That's eight times across the pool."

Riley got ready on the starting blocks. Mr. Casey walked over and said, "Remember, pace yourself. Go easy at first. Save your energy so you can get through the whole race."

When the race began, Riley jumped off to a fast start. He took the early lead in the race. Then he remembered Mr. Casey's words. Near the end of the first length, he slowed down a little bit, trying to save his energy.

He was wearing goggles, so as he swam, he could see where the other swimmers were. By the end of the third length, Riley was in last place.

This doesn't make any sense, he thought. *I'm way behind!*

He just kept going, though. At the end of the fourth length, Riley suddenly felt something change. He had developed a long, smooth stroke. His legs kicked easily. He was in a good rhythm with his strokes and his breathing. He felt relaxed.

Soon, he was catching up to the other swimmers. Even better, it didn't feel like he was really trying.

In the second to last length, Riley decided to speed up a little. His stroke stayed smooth. By the middle of the last length, Riley had passed everyone. He had won!

Riley climbed out of the pool. Mr. Casey walked over and slapped him on the back. "See?" Mr. Casey said, smiling. "I told you you'd be a good long-distance swimmer."

"You were right, Mr. Casey," Riley said. "That was awesome."

Blake walked over. "Nice job," he said to Riley. "I was a little worried there for a while. You were way behind! But you definitely pulled ahead at the end."

"I have a question for you guys," Mr. Casey said. "Have you ever thought about going out for the swim team? Blake, you'd be great at sprint races. And Riley, you'd be perfect for longer races."

Riley raised his eyebrows. It did sound pretty cool. But before he could say anything, Blake laughed.

"Thanks, but we're not interested," Blake said. "Riley and I aren't really into school sports and that kind of stuff. Right, Riley?"

"Um, I guess," Riley said.

Mr. Casey looked disappointed, but he just shrugged. "All right," he said. "Maybe next year, then." He walked away.

CHAPTER 5

THERE'S STILL TIME

After school, Riley and Blake walked home together. "Are you sure you don't want to be on the swim team?" Riley asked. "It could be fun."

Blake looked at him and laughed. "Are you kidding me?" he said. "The only thing more boring than gym has to be swim team practice. I've seen those guys. All they do is swim back and forth. For hours. Besides, who wants to hang around a bunch of jocks, anyway?"

"Okay, okay," Riley said. "Forget I asked."

"Speaking of swimming, do you want to go back to the cliffs again this Saturday?" Blake asked. "We could do the jump again. Only this time, maybe you'll learn how to land instead of doing a belly flop on your back." He laughed.

Riley felt a nervous, sick feeling in the pit of his stomach. *I never want to go back there,* he thought. But he looked at Blake and smiled. "Yeah, sounds great," Riley said. "I'll definitely be there."

* * *

On Friday morning, Mr. Casey asked Riley to stay after class. After he showered and changed back into his normal clothes, Riley found Mr. Casey in his office.

"I want to talk to you about the swim team," Mr. Casey said. "I know Blake doesn't want to join, but I thought I'd ask you again." He paused, and then added, "You know, you don't have to listen to him about everything."

Riley frowned. "I don't listen to him about everything," he said. "I do what I want."

"Well, I hope you'll think about joining the team," Mr. Casey said. "It's a lot of fun. You would be very good at it. And the other guys are really great."

"Blake's a good guy too," Riley replied.

"I know he is," Mr. Casey said. "I'd like Blake to join the team too. If he's not interested, that's okay. I just want to make sure you're making this decision on your own."

Riley looked down at the floor. "Yes, I am," he said.

"Okay," Mr. Casey said. "But just in case, practice starts Monday after school. So there's still time to change your mind."

Riley nodded. "Okay, thanks," he said.

CHAPTER 6

On Saturday morning, Riley headed to the cliff at Lake Owens. Blake was already in the parking lot when Riley arrived. He was talking to a group of older guys Riley recognized from school. He wasn't friends with those guys. They were the kind of kids who were always in trouble or in detention.

"Hey, Riley," Blake said as Riley walked up. "Guys, this is the kid I was telling you about — the one who landed flat on his back in the water last week."

All the older guys laughed. Riley turned red, but he tried to shrug it off. After all, he was used to Blake making fun of him sometimes.

"This guy actually wanted to join the swim team," Blake went on. "Can you imagine? I would hate to be friends with a dumb jock, especially one on the swim team."

The older guys laughed again. "Yeah, the jocks are the worst," one of them said. "I can't stand them."

"Let's get up to the cliff," Blake said.

Everyone turned and headed toward the base of the hill. "You're going to jump, right?" Blake asked Riley as they walked. "You can't embarrass me in front of these guys. I told them you were cool."

Riley shrugged. "I don't really feel like jumping," he said. "I might just get right in the water."

Blake shook his head. "At least come up to the top of the cliff with us," he said. "Seriously, these guys won't let us hang out with them if you act like a loser."

"Fine," Riley said. "Whatever."

They climbed to the top of the cliff. One by one, the older guys all jumped, landing in the water far below. Soon, just Blake and Riley were left standing on the cliff.

Riley peered over the edge. Then he looked at Blake, standing a few feet behind him.

"You can go ahead," Riley said. "Maybe I'll wait until everyone comes up and jumps again."

"No way, man!" Blake said. "You're just trying to get out of jumping. Go ahead, go!"

Riley sighed. "Look, I really don't want to," he said.

Blake looked at him. After a moment, he said, "Okay, fine." He stepped toward the edge of the cliff. Riley moved to get out of his friend's way, but as he did, Blake's arm swung out. With all his strength, he pushed Riley off the edge of the cliff.

CHAPTER 7

SOMETHING NEW

Sputtering for air, Riley came up to the water's surface. All the other guys crowded around him, laughing. "Blake had to push him in," one of them said.

Riley felt his face turn hot. He swam toward the edge of the lake.

Blake jumped off the cliff and landed in the water nearby. When he popped his head out of the water, he was laughing.

"Where are you going, Riley?" Blake asked. "I know you're not jumping again, since you needed a push to jump in the first place." He swam toward Riley, smiling.

"Don't talk to me," Riley said angrily. "I'm going home."

Blake looked surprised. "Why?" he asked. "I was just having a little fun."

"Well, it wasn't fun," Riley said. "Seriously. I could have been hurt, or worse. You can't just push people in like that!" he yelled.

Riley looked over Blake's shoulder. The older guys were watching them, laughing.

"Come on, Blake," one of them yelled. "We're going up to the cliff again. Let your little friend go home and cry to his mommy."

Blake looked at Riley for a second. Then he turned around and swam back toward the older guys.

* * *

Riley and Blake didn't talk for the rest of the weekend. On Monday morning, they avoided each other in gym class. Riley didn't bother trying to talk to Blake.

After school that day, Riley found himself in a line of people signing up for the swim team.

Mr. Casey smiled when he saw Riley in the line. "It's great to see you here, Riley," Mr. Casey said. "What made you change your mind?"

Riley looked down at the ground. "Let's just say I wanted to try something new," he said quietly.

Mr. Casey nodded. "Well, whatever got you here," he said, "I'm glad to see you. You're going to have fun. Where's your buddy Blake? I was hoping he'd join the team too."

Riley took a deep breath. Then he said, "I don't know what he's up to today. We've kind of gone in different directions."

"Fair enough," Mr. Casey said. "I'm glad you're here. Let's head to practice."

CHAPTER 8

THE FIRST MEET

It didn't take long for Riley to make some friends on the swim team. And it didn't take long for him to see why Mr. Casey was so excited to have him there. Before long, Riley loved the swim team.

There were a lot of very good swimmers on the team. When they worked on special strokes, like the breaststroke, backstroke, or butterfly, Riley was amazed at how good some of the other swimmers were.

When they worked on the freestyle, Riley could see there were two big holes on the team. There were several guys who could swim the middle distances well. Those were the 100-yard and 200-yard races.

The problem was, there wasn't a great sprinter on the team for the 50-yard races. And most of the swimmers got tired before they finished the 400-yard races. The team needed a sprinter and a long-distance swimmer.

Riley decided he wanted to become the long-distance swimmer on the team. It took him some time in practice to work up to the 400-yard distance, but soon, no one could beat him. At the last practice before the first meet of the season, Riley won the 400-yard race by almost a full length of the pool.

"Now you see why I wanted you on the team," Mr. Casey said after practice. "You were exactly what we needed. It's just too bad we couldn't convince Blake to join the team. We need a sprinter, too. Do you think he'd change his mind now that you're on the team?"

"I don't talk to him much," Riley said.

* * *

The first swim meet was at another school on the other side of town. Riley felt nervous. The 400-yard race was one of the last events at the meet. The longer he waited, the more nervous he felt.

He watched the other swimmers in their events. His team was doing really well, but the meet was close — Riley knew he had to do well so that his team had a chance to win.

Before the 400-yard race began, Riley shook his legs out to keep his muscles loose. He stretched and re-stretched. Finally, it was time to step up on the blocks.

All the other swimmers on the team cheered as Riley got into position in the blocks. He smiled and waved at his team.

I can't let them down, he thought.

When the horn sounded, Riley pushed himself off of the blocks and flew toward the water. His body hit the pool, and he felt all of his nervousness wash away. He was where he belonged.

Riley knew what he had to do to win the race. Just like in gym class, he started out slowly. He didn't pay attention to the other swimmers. He just got comfortable in the water.

His stroke was long and smooth. His legs pumped evenly. He felt strong as he pushed through the water. Soon, he sped up.

After the first four lengths of the race, Riley was in third place. He was only about a half-length behind the leader. As the race wore on, he sped up more and more. He concentrated on keeping his stroke long and smooth.

With four lengths to go, Riley was in second place. He moved closer to the leader of the race. He knew it was time to really speed up.

Riley kicked harder. He sped up his stroke slightly. But the swimmer in first place was an experienced swimmer. Every time Riley sped up, the other swimmer sped up too. No matter what, Riley stayed in second place.

When there were two lengths of the pool left, Riley decided he couldn't wait any longer. He used all of his strength. He caught up to the other swimmer by the final turn. When he pushed off the wall for the last length, he was slightly ahead.

Riley and the other swimmer raced to the touch pad at the end of the race. But Riley got there first.

He popped out of the water and took a deep breath. He had won his first race!

"Wooo!" his teammates called. "Great race!"

Mr. Casey grabbed Riley's hand and helped him out of the pool. Then the rest of the team came over to congratulate him.

For the first time, Riley was the center of attention. He was a winner.

CHAPTER 9

On the team bus back to their own school, Mr. Casey stood in front of the bus.

"That was a great meet," he said. "We still have a lot to work on, but we did really well. I'm proud that we won our first meet of the season, and you guys should be proud too."

The boys on the bus cheered and clapped. Riley smiled.

"On Saturday, we're going to have a team cookout," Mr. Casey continued. "It will be a good chance to just hang out and have a good time as a team. I'll pass out permission slips for you to take home to your parents."

"Where's the party going to be?" someone asked.

"It's going to be at Lake Owens," Mr. Casey said.

Riley felt sick to his stomach. If the cookout was Saturday at Lake Owens, that meant that Blake and his new friends might be there.

Riley tried to tell himself that it wouldn't matter. *He's not going to be hanging around us*, Riley thought. *We'll be by the picnic area, and he'll be over by the cliff. No big deal. He won't even know we're there.*

Still, he couldn't stop feeling worried.

* * *

On Saturday morning, Riley was still nervous. He had been avoiding Blake for several weeks, even in the one class they shared. The last thing he wanted to do was run into him, especially at Lake Owens.

All of the swim team members arrived at the lake around lunchtime. There was no one else at the picnic area. Riley relaxed a little. He ate a hamburger and played Frisbee with some of his new friends.

After about half an hour, a group of guys walked past the picnic area. Riley recognized them right away. It was Blake and his new friends. They were heading toward the cliffs, carrying towels and a cooler.

Riley tried to look away, but Blake spotted him. Blake stopped walking and looked at Riley.

"Look, it's that weird guy you used to be friends with," one of Blake's friends said.

Blake laughed. "Yeah, used to be," he said. He looked at Riley. "So, what are you, some kind of dumb jock now?" Blake yelled, loud enough for everyone to hear.

Riley didn't say a word. He felt his face turn hot.

"Having fun with the dumb jocks?" Blake continued. His friends laughed. "I didn't know dumb jocks had picnics," he added.

Riley turned away. He thought of a million things he could say, but he didn't say them.

After a minute, Blake and his friends continued walking toward the cliff, laughing and talking loudly.

Riley tried to forget they were there. But every once in a while that afternoon, he'd look up at them on the cliff. Sometimes he'd look just in time to see Blake jump into the water.

It seemed like Blake was trying new stunts as he jumped. Once, Riley saw Blake jump backward off the cliff. His friends all cheered.

Mr. Casey walked up to Riley. "I see why you don't spend much time with Blake anymore," the coach said. "Someone who acts like that isn't a friend. You should be proud of yourself for knowing you didn't have to hang around him."

"Thanks," Riley muttered. But he wasn't so sure he believed his coach.

He looked at the cliff. Blake was leaping off the cliff. His friends, waiting in the water, cheered.

Riley gasped. Blake was diving, headfirst, into the lake.

Blake hit the water. One of his friends screamed.

Riley stepped past Mr. Casey to try to get a better look. He couldn't tell what was going on, but he could tell from all the splashing that something was wrong.

There was no time to waste. Riley tore off his shirt and ran down the beach toward the water. He dove in.

A few of the other swimmers on Riley's team had seen Blake's dive too. Some people ran down the beach toward the cliff. But Riley knew the fastest way to get to Blake would be to swim.

Even though he was panicking, Riley kept his swimmer's stroke long and smooth. His legs kicked evenly. He moved quickly in Blake's direction.

Riley's steady pace helped him cover the distance very quickly. Finally, he reached Blake.

Riley swam up to Blake and eased him out of the grip of two of the older guys. "I've got him," he said.

Blake's eyes were closed. But Riley could feel Blake's heart beating, and he was breathing.

He was tired from the long swim, but Riley was still able to tug Blake back to shore. There, he gently rested Blake on the sand.

Blake moaned in pain. His right arm looked twisted. Riley saw that there was a big bump on the right side of Blake's head. The bump was bleeding.

Blake blinked and slowly moved his arms and legs. Riley smiled. That meant Blake wasn't paralyzed.

Soon the other swim team members arrived. Mr. Casey was with them. "I called 911," he said. "There's an ambulance on its way."

When Blake was loaded into the ambulance, Riley jumped in. A paramedic stopped him.

"You can't ride with us," the paramedic said. "But don't worry, it looks like your friend is going to be fine. He just hurt his shoulder. We're just taking him in to be sure, but it looks like he was really lucky."

Riley looked down at Blake. "You're going to be okay," Riley said.

"Thanks, dude," Blake said. "I guess you're not a dumb jock after all. Your swimming really helped me out. Thanks."

Riley smiled. "If you'd joined the swim team too, this never would have happened," he said.

Blake smiled back. Then he said, "Maybe it's not too late."

ABOUT THE AUTHOR

Bob Temple lives in Rosemount, Minnesota, with his wife and three children. He has written more than thirty books for children. Over the years, he has coached more than twenty kids' soccer, basketball, and baseball teams. He also loves visiting classrooms to talk about his writing.

ABOUT THE ILLUSTRATOR

When Sean Tiffany was growing up, he lived on a small island off the coast of Maine. Every day, from sixth grade until he graduated from high school, he had to take a boat to get to school. When Sean isn't working on his art, he works on a multimedia project called "OilCan Drive," which combines music and art. He has a pet cactus named Jim.

GLOSSARY

cautious (KAW-shuhss)—if you are cautious, you try to avoid mistakes or danger

courage (KUR-ij)—bravery or fearlessness

dangerous (DAYN-jur-uhss)—not safe

energy (EN-ur-jee)—strength to do things

freestyle (FREE-stile)—in swimming, any front stroke

jock (JOK)—a slang term for an athlete

pace (PAYSS)—rate of speed. If you are told to pace yourself, you are being told to keep a steady rate of speed and not use all of your energy right away.

paramedic (pa-ruh-MED-ik)—an emergency medical worker

rhythm (RITH-uhm)—a regular beat

sprint (SPRINT)—a fast race over a short distance

stroke (STROHK)—a method of moving in swimming

WATER SAFETY RULES

Always remember to SWIM SAFE.

Sharpen your skills. Take lessons and get comfortable in the water.

Watch the weather. Before you go swimming, check the weather forecast. Stop swimming in bad weather.

Investigate the area. Look around for potential dangers, like currents, deep and shallow areas, and rocks. Always be aware of your surroundings.

Monitor yourself. Are you too hot? Find some shade, reapply sunscreen, and drink some water. Are you too cold? Get out of the water and dry off. Are you too tired? Take a break from swimming and have a snack.

Stay in supervised areas. Only swim in areas that have a lifeguard on duty.

Always buddy-up. Never swim alone!

Follow the rules. Read all posted signs and obey the lifeguards.

Enter the water feet first. Only get in head first when the area is clearly marked for diving.

Although the beach and the pool are places to relax, they can also be dangerous. It's important to know basic water safety rules. Swim safe!

DISCUSSION QUESTIONS

1. When Mr. Casey first asks Blake and Riley to join the swim team, does Riley want to join? Explain your answer.

2. Why did Blake push Riley off the cliff at Lake Owens?

3. Riley doesn't like sports, but he likes swimming. What are some other ways that people can stay active, even if they don't want to join a sports team?

WRITING PROMPTS

1. Have you ever had an argument with a close friend? What happened? How did you resolve the problem? Write about it.

2. Riley decides to join the swim team even though Blake doesn't. Write about a time when you did something that your friends didn't think was cool.

3. At the end of this book, Blake has to go to the hospital. What do you think happens next? Write a story that begins when this book ends.

Joe spends too much time trying to wow the crowd, and not enough time helping the team. At tryouts for the freshman team, Joe is quickly cut. He needs to stop fooling around and prove he has what it takes to stay in the game.

Juan can't catch, he can't throw, and one of the members of the football team hasn't been making it easy for Juan to feel at home. Can the ex-track star learn his new sport in time for the biggest game of the season?

INTERNET SITES

Do you want to know more about subjects related to this book? Or are you interested in learning about other topics? Then check out FactHound, a fun, easy way to find Internet sites.

Our investigative staff has already sniffed out great sites for you!

Here's how to use FactHound:

1. Visit *www.facthound.com*

2. Select your grade level.

3. To learn more about subjects related to this book, type in the book's ISBN number: **9781434212054**.

4. Click the **Fetch It** button.

FactHound will fetch the best Internet sites for you!